KROOPENPOPPER

An Everglades Adventure

Virginia Saalman

By **Virginia Saalman**

Illustrated by **Pattie Tedesco Jones**

Moson Publishing
NAPLES, FLORIDA

Published by

MoSon Publishing
NAPLES, FLORIDA

www.adventurebooksforchildren.net

Summary: The first in a series of Kroopenpopper adventures. Mary and Tommy Kroopenpopper, accompanied by Mr. Bear, venture deep into the Everglades to find the home of the squirrel family. The animals of the swamp help the children escape the clutches of the feared Night-flying Woofing Bird?

First Paperback Edition: November 2009 - ISBN: 978-0-9821938-0-8

Library of Congress Control Number: 2009938140

Preface

Before life's experiences invade and clutter young minds, imagination can propel a child to places where fantasy is alive, monsters are slain, and miracles happen. The Everglades is not a place for two children unfamiliar with the dangers that lurk within. Mary and Tommy Kroopenpopper let caution give way to curiosity as they followed Mr. Bear deep into the Florida Everglades.

Daylight will soon disappear behind the moss-laden trees. The silence of the hot, lazy afternoon will be replaced with the night sounds of the great cypress swamp. The watery woods will come alive with persistent noisemakers with the limpkins leading the chorus as they shatter the night with their "kree-ow, kree-ow, kree-ow."

Some swamp people still say that they have seen or heard the shriek of the Night-flying Woofing Bird and some still believe that the eerie sound of the limpkin is the scream from an Indian child the bird was rumored to have carried away many years ago. Will the Kroopenpopper children fall into the bird's clutches?

This story is dedicated to my grandson, Tyler, who was the first to hear the story of Mary and Tommy's venture into the forest to find the home of the squirrel family, and to Tyler's younger brother, Luke, both of whom delight and who make me forget my age and how cluttered my own mind is with life experiences. This book is for them and for all children in whose imaginations fantasy comes to life and where anything is possible.

I am grateful to my family, especially my children, stepchildren, nephews and niece, who, for many years, patiently listened to the telling of the Kroopenpooper adventures. I will always be indebted to my husband, Captain Bill, for his encouragement and his knowledge of the Everglades. Thanks to my friends who edited the text. As always, special thanks go to "De" for continually encouraging the Kroopenpopper adventures to transcend my imagination to the printed page.

Without the illustrations by Pattie Tedesco, this story could live only in the imagination. Her talent gives it life.

Once upon a time, a family named Kroopenpopper lived in a small town in Maryland. There was Momma Kroopenpopper, Poppa Kroopenpopper, Mary Kroopenpopper, and Tommy Kroopenpopper. They were a happy family and every year they looked forward to summer vacation. As soon as the Christmas decorations were packed away, the tourist pamphlets came out and were carefully read. Everyone was excited when the small town of Buttonwood in the Florida Everglades was decided on. When vacation time finally came, they began the long trip south.

The yellow cottage sat on a hardwood hammock at the edge of a large cypress swamp near Buttonwood, a small town in the Florida Everglades. Tommy and Mary enjoyed swinging on their swings or lying on their mother's colorful quilt as they watched clouds move across the blue sky. They loved being close to the woods and they spent hours watching for the critters they had read about earlier.

After a couple of weeks, they were disappointed that they hadn't seen any wildlife at all, except the usual evening invasion of fireflies, mosquitoes, and a few squirrels that always appeared suddenly, scampered frantically about, dug in the dirt, romped in the leaves, and then, just as suddenly, ran away.

"We need to go into the woods to see animals," Tommy told Mary one day when he didn't think their mother could hear.

"I heard that, young man," their mother said, as she pointed her finger at Tommy. "Don't ever go far away from the house without Poppa or me! The swamp can be very dangerous and you can easily get lost."

A few days later, when Tommy and Mary were playing on the swings, Mary asked Tommy if he knew where the squirrels lived.

"In trees somewhere, I guess," he said. "Why?"

"Well I see them every day. They come into the yard, dig and then run back into the woods."

"Probably in some big tree," Tommy added. He was swinging so high that Mary was sure he would fall and break his neck, a prediction she had heard their mother scold many times.

Just as Mary was about to scream for him to slow down, they heard a loud grunt from the nearby bushes. "What was that?" Mary asked.

"What?" Tommy said as he dragged his feet and tumbled off head first.

"That noise?"

"I didn't hear anything except the wind."

Mary stopped swinging and looked toward the bush. "It wasn't the wind. I heard something."

"You're always hearing something," Tommy said. "Remember when you heard a giraffe outside your bedroom window?"

"I did," she said. "You never believe me."

"Giraffes are usually very quiet," Tommy told her with some authority. "And besides, they *don't* live in the Everglades."

"Well this giraffe does," Mary said, jumping off her swing and landing on her knees.

"Ouch, that hurt," she said, brushing off her pants.

Just then they both heard the noise. It was louder and closer. They froze in place, not daring to move. Suddenly, they saw a big, hairy head, followed by the black body of the largest bear they had ever seen. But, of course, it was the only *real* bear they had *ever* seen.

They had seen a bear on a poster in the National Park in Bighorn Canyon in Montana. **"Don't Feed the Bears!"** that sign warned.

The bushes parted. The huge animal moved in their direction. Tommy grabbed Mary's hand. "Don't move," he said.

"Hello," the bear said. "Don't be afraid; I'm a friend from the swamp."

"Don't say anything," Tommy said. "Bears will eat you alive. Remember what Momma said."

The big bear moved closer and stood on his hind legs, towering over the frightened children. "I've never eaten anything but berries, honey, grass roots, and an occasional armadillo, and I resent that comment."

"He's taller than Poppa," Mary whispered. "And Poppa's over six feet tall."

"S-h-h-h," Tommy said. "Maybe he'll go away if we ignore him."

The bear was soon standing so close that they could feel the warmth of his breath and see the sheen of his long, coarse coat ---- AND ---- they could see the size of his LONG and SHARP front claws!!

"Sorry if I frightened you," the bear said. "I couldn't help hearing you as you played on the swings."

Sure that any minute they would become the animal's dinner, Mary decided to act friendly and unafraid. "Oh, that's OK," she said. "We weren't afraid at all. Were we Tommy?"

"No," he said, with a shaky voice and a quivering lower jaw. "Not at all!"

"Good," the huge animal said." "Let's take a walk into the cypress swamp. I know a secret trail."

"Oh, we couldn't do that," Mary said. "We're not allowed. Are we, Tommy?"

"Nope, nope, nope," Tommy said. "Mommy would surely be angry if we did."

The bear scratched his head and dropped onto all fours which made him look a little less dangerous. "Hmmm," he said. "I thought you wanted to know where the squirrels live. Is that right?"

Mary jumped right in, forgetting that just moments before she almost fainted from fright at the sight of the huge animal. "That's right! Where *do* they live? Do *you* know?"

Tommy cast a warning glance at Mary, but curiosity kept him from saying anything.

"No, but somebody in the swamp must know," the big, black animal said. "Would you like to come with me and find out?"

Their excitement overtook all caution and Tommy and Mary both jumped up and down at the same time.

"Yes! Yes! Yes!" they said with great enthusiasm.

So Mary, Tommy, and the bear began walking down the trail deep into the swamp. Cypress knees stuck up from the black water.

"What should we call you?" Mary asked as she and Tommy took large steps to keep up. "Bear? Black Bear? Or what?"

"Mr. Bear," he said. "Mr. Bear will do nicely."

They soon reached the side of a creek where a small doe was drinking water.

"Hello, Mrs. Deer!" Mr. Bear shouted. "We're going to find where the squirrels live. Do you happen to know?"

"No," said Mrs. Deer. "But if you like, I'll walk with you and try to find them."

"That would be nice," said Mr. Bear.

So Mary, Tommy, and Mr. Bear, followed by Mrs. Deer, began to walk down the trail to find where the squirrels lived.

They came to another creek where a beaver was busy building a dam. A pileated woodpecker hammered away on the trunk of a tall pine.

SMACK! The sound of the beaver's tail, as it crashed on the water.

"Hello, Mr. Beaver!" Mr. Bear shouted. "We're going to find where the squirrels live. Do you happen to know?"

"No," said Mr. Beaver, as he shook the water from his large tail. "But I'd be glad to go along, but only if you walk slowly 'cause this big, old tail works better in water than on land."

"Promise," they all said at once.

So Mary, Tommy, and Mr. Bear, followed by Mrs. Deer and Mr. Beaver, began to walk down the trail to find where the squirrels lived.

They soon noticed a long, green snake that was slithering along the trail which, in some places, was wet and squishy.

"Hello, Mr. Snake!" shouted Mr. Bear. "We're taking a walk to find where the squirrels live. Do you happen to know?"

"No," said Mr. Snake. "But if you like, I'll come with you and try to find them."

"That would be nice," said Mr. Bear.

So Mary, Tommy, and Mr. Bear, followed by Mrs. Deer, Mr. Beaver, and Mr. Snake, began to walk, or rather slink in the case of Mr. Snake, down the trail to find where the squirrels lived.

The trail opened onto a hammock where native royal palms, cabbage palms, and hog plum trees reached toward the sky. A small brown and white chipmunk scampered back and forth across the path.

"Hello, Mrs. Chipmunk!" shouted Mr. Bear. "We're taking a walk to find where the squirrels live. Do you happen to know?"

"No," said Mrs. Chipmunk. "But if you like, I'll come with you and try to find them."

"That would be nice," said Mr. Bear.

So Mary, Tommy, and Mr. Bear, followed by Mrs. Deer, Mr. Beaver, Mr. Snake, and Mrs. Chipmunk, began to walk down the path to find where the squirrels lived.

They soon reached a clearing on the side of the path where a big, fawn-colored panther was sound asleep.

"Hello, Mr. Panther!" shouted the bear, loud enough to wake the sleeping animal. "We're taking a walk to find where the squirrels live. Do you happen to know?"

"No," said Mr. Panther. "But since you awakened me from my nap, I'll come with you and try to find them."

"That would be nice," said Mr. Bear.

So Mary, Tommy, and Mr. Bear, followed by Mrs. Deer, Mr. Beaver, Mr. Snake, Mrs. Chipmunk, and the sleepy Panther, began to walk down the trail to find where the squirrels lived. They passed another small pond where a big, crusty alligator was napping in the hot sun. Wading birds feeding on mosquitofish, and an old turtle, too lazy to move, were no help.

Suddenly, they heard a roaring cry from the trees overhead. Mary and Tommy covered their ears and looked up. Just as they did, a large monkey came swinging down fast from high overhead, branch to branch. It landed abruptly in front of the children, its sharp eyes peering intently from its black face.

"Hello, Mr. Howler Monkey," Mr. Bear said. "I thought the zoo would have found you long ago."

"No way," said the monkey. "They'll never find me and I'm never going back."

Mary and Tommy looked at Mr. Bear for an explanation.

Mr. Bear leaned over and spoke as quietly as a four-hundred pound black bear could.

"You mustn't tell anyone about this."

"We promise," Mary said. "But why?"

"He escaped from the zoo two years ago during the hurricane, and all the animals in the swamp protect him. The humans haven't found him yet. Now let's hurry."

Mr. Bear then turned to the monkey and said, "We're going to find where the squirrels live. Do you want to come with us?"

"Yes," said the monkey. "I'll go along and help you find them."

"That would be nice," said Mr. Bear. "But you must promise to be very quiet." Mr. Monkey raised his right arm and promised.

"Why must he be quiet?" Mary asked.

"Because," Mr. Bear explained. "Mr. Monkey is louder than any other animal in the swamp, even louder than the roar of Mr. Lion and Mr. Tiger.

"Gosh," Tommy said. "If the zoo people are looking for him, he must be very careful, right?"

"Exactly," said Mr. Bear. "Now let's get going before it begins to get dark. We need a lot of light to find the squirrels' home."

And so Mary, Tommy, and Mr. Bear, followed by Mrs. Deer, Mr. Beaver, Mr. Snake, Mrs. Chipmunk, Mr. Panther, and the *very* quiet Mr. Monkey, walked down the trail to find where the squirrels lived.

As they moved, an animal with a long neck, short legs, and short horn-like stubs on his head, slowly stepped onto the trail in front of the group.

Mary screeched with delight. "I told you!" she said. I told you!"

Tommy couldn't believe what he was seeing. It *was* a giraffe – of all things!

"Hello, Mrs. Giraffe!" shouted Mr. Bear. "We're going to find where the squirrels live. Do you happen to know?"

"No," said Mrs. Giraffe. "But I know someone who does know. He is very wise and he will tell you where they live. May I come along with you?"

"Of course," said Mr. Bear.

So Mary and Tommy, followed by Mr. Bear, Mrs. Deer, Mr. Beaver, Mr. Snake, Mrs. Chipmunk, Mr. Panther, the *very* quiet Mr. Monkey, and the *very* tall Mrs. Giraffe, walked deeper into the swamp to locate the home of the squirrels.

The group hadn't walked very far when they heard a noise that sounded like a dog barking and a rooster crowing. *"Who cooks for you all?" "Who cooks for you all?"*

The line of animals stopped quickly, each bumping into the one in front.

"What's that?" Mary asked.

"Oh that," said Mr. Bear. "That's my friend, Mr. Barred Owl. He's the wisest of all the creatures in the swamp."

"But I'm the loudest," said Mr. Monkey.

"And I'm the tallest," said Mrs. Giraffe.

"Hello, Mr. Barred Owl," said Mr. Bear. "What are you doing awake? It's daytime and you are always asleep during the day."

"Yes," said Mr. Owl. "I'm nocturnal which, of course, you know means I sleep during the day and go about my business during the night. But with all the noise you're making, even a hibernating bear – which, of course, you know means a bear sleeping all winter – couldn't sleep."

Mr. Bear lowered his head. "I'm sorry, Mr. Owl, but you see, we've been walking a long time to find the home of the squirrels."

Soon all the animals were chiming in. "Yes, we're so sorry to wake you, but we really want to find out where the squirrels live. Can you help us?"

"Of course," said Mr. Owl. "I know everything there is to know in the swamp. Earl and Pearl Squirrel are friends of mine. Since it will be dark in a few hours, I might as well go along. Follow me," he commanded and he spread his large wings and flew down the trail ahead of the long line of animals.

"And hurry!" he said. "It will get dark early and the squirrels are just having afternoon tea, pinecones, and nuts and they are expecting us."

Mary and Tommy ran to keep up with Mr. Owl.

"Hurry, Tommy!" Mary yelled to her brother. "We're *really* going to find out where the squirrels live. Hurry!"

Down on all fours, Mr. Bear loped ahead.

Mrs. Deer ran and jumped over Mr. Bear.

Mr. Beaver's big tail was dragging the ground and slowing him down.

Mr. Snake yelled as the others ran down the path in front of him. "Wait! Wait! You think I've got legs?"

Mrs. Chipmunk ran as fast as her little body would let her.

Mr. Panther moved swiftly, silently, and low to the ground. He didn't seem to be exerting any effort at all.

Mr. Monkey used his long arms to propel himself from branch to branch, and Mrs. Giraffe lengthened her stride so that she could run faster.

Mr. Owl came to a full stop on a low-hanging branch at the edge of a beautiful, grassy circle surrounded by big oak trees. Tommy and Mary, panting and out of breath, arrived at the edge of the clearing at the same time as Mr. Snake.

The excited animals gathered together and whispered. A majestic oak tree, with moss hanging from its branches, stood in the middle of the clearing. Mary and Tommy couldn't believe their eyes.

A large table was covered with vines that cascaded over the sides and onto the benches. Mary and Tommy and all animals became very still with the wonder of it all. They had finally found the home of the squirrels and it was a magical sight.

It was then that Mary first saw the tiny figure with the golden hair and delicate wings who had been watching over them from the very moment they started down the trail. Just as Mary began to tell the others what she had seen, the swamp fairy darted behind a large leaf. At that very moment, Mr. Owl looked down and announced that, indeed, they had arrived at the home of Pearl and Earl Squirrel, and Mary forgot, until later, what she had seen.

"Come in everyone," Mr. Owl said, as he flew down from the branch and over to the big door at the base of the tree. "A magnificent Quercus Virginiana," he proclaimed loudly. The animals all looked at one another. They had never heard of a Quercus Virginiana. Mr. Owl was very wise and didn't mind everyone knowing it. "It's a Live Oak, of course," he said with much authority, as if all should have known.

Mary and Tommy, Mr. Bear, Mrs. Deer, Mr. Beaver, Mrs. Chipmunk, Mr. Panther, Mr. Monkey, and Mrs. Giraffe slowly moved toward the big table. Poor Mr. Snake; he was so slow he hadn't yet caught up with the others. Mr. Owl flapped his wings and pecked on the door.

The massive, wooden door swung open. All the animals sighed. They couldn't believe it. They had finally found where the squirrels lived and were actually going to have tea and nuts with them.

Mr. Squirrel came out first to greet the animals, followed by Mrs. Squirrel who carried hickory nuts, acorns, and pinecones in the fold of her apron.

"Welcome friends! Welcome," Mr. Squirrel said, as he placed a pot of tea and a large bowl of swamp cabbage on the table. "What kept you so long? We heard you were coming; we've been waiting."

"Sit! Sit!" commanded Mrs. Squirrel, as she emptied the contents of her apron on the table and placed nuts and acorns in front of the seated guests.

All the animals turned and looked at Mr. Snake who, having finally arrived, dropped his head and slithered up onto one of the chairs. He looked around at everyone. "It's not my fault I don't have legs, thank you all very much," he said indignantly. "And quite frankly," he added. "I'm glad I don't have them – legs, that is – because then, I wouldn't be a snake, would I?" Everyone nodded and laughed.

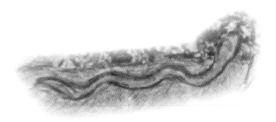

As soon as Pearl and Earl Squirrel sat down, two little squirrels appeared on a branch overhead. They giggled and frolicked so much that they both came tumbling down, smack into the middle of the table, scattering all the goodies.

"Children!" Mrs. Squirrel scolded, her tail twitching madly up and down. "Mind your manners; we have company."

Merle and Burl Squirrel did as they were told. They had never seen so many animals in one place, and were quite delighted that they were allowed to sit at the big table, but only, their mother said, if they were very polite. Even though it was difficult for the young squirrels, they were *very* quiet and they *did* mind their manners.

It was a wonderful afternoon with Mary, Tommy, and all of the animals of the swamp talking, laughing, and enjoying the feast. Mr. Beaver made everyone giggle when he tried to crack open the hickory nuts by slamming them with his large tail.

Just then, Mary looked up and noticed that the sunshine had disappeared behind the large trees. "My goodness, Tommy," she said. "It's getting dark and we have a long way to go." Night was starting to fall.

Mrs. Squirrel stood up, twitching her long gray tail. "You're right," she said. "You must leave now! It's rumored that the evil Night-Flying Woofing Bird has returned to the forest." The children and the animals got very quiet. Everyone turned to the wise owl for an explanation.

"It's true," Mr. Owl said. "I heard it just this morning. The children must leave immediately." Frightened, Mary and Tommy jumped up and began to run toward the trail.

"Wait!" called Mr. Owl. "You'll never make it before dark if you walk. My wings are big enough for you to ride upon, but they are much too light to hold you. I'm afraid I can't carry you." He looked toward Mr. Bear.

"I'm too slow," said Mr. Bear, and he looked at Mrs. Deer.

"I jump much too high to safely carry both of you," said Mrs. Deer, and she looked at Mr. Beaver.

"Goodness sakes," Mr. Beaver said. "With this tail, you really think I could get them home before dark?" He looked toward Mr. Snake.

"Get real," Mr. Snake yelled. "Besides, I won't even get there myself before tomorrow morning. It's obvious to anyone with eyes that I'm the slowest one here." He looked toward Mr. Monkey

"I'd do it," Mr. Monkey said. "But I go really fast as I swing through the tops of trees. I'd probably drop them." He looked at Mrs. Giraffe.

"Oh, I wish I could," said Mrs. Giraffe, as she looked toward Mr. Owl. "But with this long neck, they'd most assuredly fall off and break their own necks."

"Being the wise one of the group, there's only one option here that I can see," said Mr. Owl, and he looked directly at Mr. Panther.

Without even thinking long about it, Mr. Panther jumped up and rushed to Tommy and Mary.

"Mr. Owl is right and *very* wise," the panther said. "I can do it. Hop on quickly and hold on tight!"

Tommy and Mary *did* jump on Mr. Panther, barely having a moment to look back and thank Mr. and Mrs. Squirrel again before the powerful animal leaped into action and charged across the clearing and down the trail.

"Hang on, Mary!" Tommy screamed. "Hang on!"

Half way down the trail, the air became cool, and darkness settled over the forest. From high above, there came a screech like nothing the Kroopenpopper children had ever heard. Closer and closer!

Mr. Panther yelled: "It's him! The Night-Flying Woofing Bird, and he's heading this way. I must run faster and faster and hope that the fairies of the forest are close. The Woofing Bird fears nothing but the swamp fairies."

"You mean there really is a Night-Flying Woofing Bird? And fairies?" Mary yelled. But the panther was moving too fast through the dim light to hear her. Down the trail, past the pond, the sleek animal raced. Mary looked over her shoulder. Suddenly, it was so close she could almost touch it. Eyes burning red, yellow drool streaming from its beak and long, sharp, yellow talons stretching out toward them. "W-o-o-o-f!" it shrieked. "W-o-o-o-f!"

The panther darted back and forth to keep the children from being snatched off his back. Closer and closer the bird came and just as it was about to grab a child in each foot, a band of fairies descended from the tree. One by one they attacked the Woofing Bird, who, just as Mr. Owl had predicted, retreated quickly into the dark swamp. And, just as suddenly, the fairies and Mr. Panther disappeared also. The air became warm once again.

As if by magic, the two Kroopenpopper children found themselves safely back in the yard of their home. Tommy was lying on the colorful quilt, and Mary was leaning against a tree, sound asleep. They awakened to the sound of their mother's voice, as she called from inside the cottage.

"I hope you didn't fall asleep on that blanket," she said. "Remember what I told you; all manner of creatures could have come into the yard and gobbled you up."

Tommy and Mary looked at each other, and then quickly scrambled onto the grass. They watched without speaking as their mother gathered the corners of the quilt and shook off the nuts, acorns, and pinecones.

"Oh yes, Mommy," Mary said."

"We remembered." Tommy said.

"Good, now come get washed up for dinner."

Mary and Tommy glanced toward the edge of the swamp. Did they really see a pair of large yellow eyes and a slight movement in the bushes? Was that the sound of tiny wings high above or was it their imaginations?

The End